GILBERT LUIS R. CENTINA III

MADRE ESPAÑA
AND
ILLUSTRATED
LOVE POEMS

Cover design concept and illustration: *Machús Aguirre*
Art consultant: *Janet Frances White*
Book interior design: *Pierce Centina*
Front cover photo of Javier Aguirre and María Jesús Salamero courtesy of the private photo collection of the Aguirre family.

Published by CentiRamo Publishing, New York, NY
www.centiramopublishing.com ❖ info@centiramopublishing.com

ISBN-13: 978-1-7327815-5-9
ISBN-10: 1-7327815-5-9

POPULAR EDITION

Library of Congress Control Number: 2019940282
l.c. record of this book may be accessed at https://lccn.loc.gov/2019940282

20 19 18 17 16 15 14 13 12 11 10 9 8 7

GILBERT LUIS R. CENTINA III

MADRE ESPAÑA
AND
ILLUSTRATED
LOVE POEMS

ILLUSTRATED BY
MACHÚS AGUIRRE

DEDICATION

For Javier Aguirre and María Jesús Salamero
(In Memoriam)

The love you planted
Has grown into a tree,
Strong, pliant, formidable
But welcoming to birds and bees.
Javier's paintings hang
Inside the chalet in Barrika
Where once a year your niece comes
To play the violin for the deer
That occupy the place reserved
For them at the slope overlooking
Sopelana Beach. Your love for God
And your desire to serve your fellowmen
Are your legacy to the whole clan.
Visiting friends see both of you in them
And fondly remember you with love
As they stir their red tea mixed with milk
To brownish gold.

CONTENTS

MADRE ESPAÑA

Contents

Contents

ILLUSTRATED LOVE POEMS

Contents

ost of the poems in the first part of this book honor the Spanish people and the great Kingdom of Spain, the Mother Country of many nations throughout the world, including the Philippines, my Southeast Asian homeland. The second part is devoted unabashedly to love, the most uniquely human of all emotions. When directed toward God, it is expressed as a prayer of thanksgiving and a way to celebrate when shared with a loved one.

As the birthplace of Hispanidad, Spain has left an indelible mark on almost half a billion people estimated to speak the Spanish language across the globe. Besides a common language, more bonds glue Spain and its former colonies together: blood, religion, history, culture and tradition, food, music, dance, and literature, to name just a few.

Like an epic, 1898 was in medias res of Spanish arts and letters. That year, the defeat of Spain in the Spanish-American War was a terrible disaster for the Spaniards. The United States of America, eager to spread its wings in the name of "Manifest Destiny," had declared war on Spain and, in a few months, the government of Spanish Prime Minister Práxedes Mariano Mateo Sagasta y Escolar lost Cuba, Puerto Rico, the Philippines, and Guam. This event gave birth to the "Generation of '98 (*Generación del 98*)," that period in Spanish arts and letters represented by José Martínez Ruiz (who wrote under the pseudonym Azorín), Miguel de Unamuno, Ramiro de Maeztu, and many other glorious writers. Some precursors who had already read the handwriting on the wall were Joaquín Costa Martinez, Ricardo Macías Picavea, Ángel Gavinet García, and Juan Bautista Amores.

The Philippines was named after King Philip II, who had said of his colony that the sun would never set on it, but soon the Spanish empire became an anachronism, out of step, out of place, breathing its last gasps. It all came to an end when Spain lost its overseas possessions.

But the loss of material possessions produced greatness. During this time in Spain, great minds were born and dominated the civilized world, illuminating the four corners of the Earth with their thought, poetry, and philosophy, using pen and palette. Modernism would replace the Age of Conquest.

This was conquest just the same, but a finer, higher kind, the triumph of spirit over flesh; the apotheosis of idea over matter. It was Granada regaining its lost grandeur, but this time with an influence more pervasive and lasting because intangible.

When the bells of the Cathedral of León and the Cathedral of Burgos pealed, the echoes reached the world's farthest corners. Artists and thinkers navigated the horizons of the human mind in a search for truth. José Ortega y Gasset was followed by Eugenio d'Ors, Gregorio Marañón, and Ramón Gómez de la Serna.

At the turn of the last century, the world would be astounded by the writings of Antonio Machado, Juan Ramón Jimenez, José María Gabriel y Galán, and Vicente Medina. Between wars blazed the stars of Juan Larrea, Gerardo Diego, Pedro Salinas, Jorge Guillén, and Dámaso Alonso.

Then Rafael Alberti, José Ma. Pemán, Federico García Lorca, Vicente Aleixandre, and Miguel Hernández made a detour for the popular recreating myths and legends, addressing the most lettered and the most pastoral. These writers were all an offshoot of Generation of '98.

Pablo Picasso, father of Cubism and considered, along with Leonardo da Vinci and Michelangelo, one of the three greatest painters of humankind, should properly belong to Generation of '98. Salvador Dali, the surrealist "super genius" whose works are "works of genius," should also properly belong to this generation.

I have lived and worked in Spain as an Augustinian friar for the past six years. I have seen up close and personal the incredible warmth and extreme kindness of the Spanish people, who think of others first before themselves. I am writing this a year to the day I underwent life-saving surgery, full of gratitude in my heart for the hospitality and the generosity of the Spanish people, which have sustained me in my long and continuing journey to recovery. Their selflessness exemplifies the nobility of their Iberian roots.

Spain's greatness did not come crashing down with the collapse of the Spanish empire. The setback simply put Spain to the test in the hot coals of adversity from which it has emerged ever more triumphant as an inextinguishable idea far beyond *plus ultra*.

— Gilbert Luis R. Centina III
June 20, 2019
Loiu, Vizcaya, Spain

MADRE ESPAÑA

In Spain, the dead are more alive than the dead of any other country in the world.

— *Federico García Lorca*

Brindis

To the world's most efficient,
Unfailing health care system:
¡Viva España!
To its delicious cuisine,
Aged brandy, finest wine:
¡Viva España!
To *jamón ibérico*,
Cecina and *chorizo*:
¡Viva España!
To *paella, merluza,*
Naranjas and *turrones.*
¡Viva España!
To José Echegaray,
Velázquez and Picasso:
¡Viva España!
To eye-popping flamenco
And *corridas de toro*:
¡Viva España!
To Cristóbal Colón, plus
Los Reyes Católicos:
¡Viva España!
To where the sun never sets
North or East or West or South:
¡Viva España!

The City

Looms this city we long for,
Singular and heavenly,
Free from strife, devoid of hate.
Carbuncles of light
Illumine its pearly gate,
Two angels with flaming sword
Guard its citadel.
When you enter this city
Only one thing is required:
Love. Present your heart,
Bring with you a heart that loves.

Gone at Dawn, the Stars

Gone at dawn, the stars
Give no light when morning comes.
They are nowhere to be seen.
Soaked in tears, the grass,
Like abandoned street children,
Miss the guidance of the stars,
Now light years away,
Traveling and pursuing
The path of the Milky Way.
Gone at dawn, the stars
Give no light when morning comes.
The weeping grass feels orphaned.

In Hellfire, False Accusers

In hellfire, false accusers
Wail in pain and gnash their teeth.
Vicious wasps and worms,
Like falsehood, they swore to tell,
Issue from their mouth,
Not one there cares to listen,
Not one has the heart
To ease the aeviternal,
Endless suffering
Of souls condemned to hellfire.

Rewind

Childhood misadventures,
Ashes in memory's crypt,
Overwhelm and confuse,
Like when with three other brats
I challenged grandfather's turkey
For a fight, the fowl stood its ground
And vigorously defended its little ones.
Uncle Dimple came to our rescue
And stoned the fowl, tried to revive
It later, but in vain; heart-rending
Chirps of orphaned chicks
Filled us with guilt afterward;
Or like the evening I tiptoed
In an area off-limits to children,
Without any rhyme or reason,
I needlessly ventured to dip
My unwashed hands into the cookie jar
The sideboard shook, in a split second
Broken chinaware came crashing down,
Grandma's precious heirloom gone.

Self-recrimination hurts the most
When the past delivers a monologue

And you are not allowed to speak
But forced to listen. Those who used
To clean up your childhood mess
Are no longer around to cuddle you
Or reassure you things will be all right.
You bite your elbow, but you cannot.
The past never makes a deal.
To remember is a real gift.
To forget is sometimes a blessing.

Things Happen

Things happen sometimes
The way we least expect them,
When we do not expect them
To happen. We see
A swarm of white dragonflies
Like shrunken voodoo airplanes,
Nosediving over our heads,
All for a show, pure optics.

Reality stuns
When life goes on to normal
At twilight; the sun leaves
No trace of its bloody death.
White dragonflies perch on boughs,
As darkness covers the earth.

End Times

Go when bright peacocks,
Their plumage ripe for courtship,
Proudly strut the earth;
When fair weather storks
With a baby at their beck
Dominate the skies;
When sharks and blue whales,
Belugas and viperfish,
Rule our coral reefs;
When ray-finned catfish
With their standard black whiskers
Disturb our rivers;
When the crocodiles,
Hungry with reptilian greed,
Overrun our streets.
Never doubting, without fear,
Go when it is time to go.

As you go, follow the light.
And don't bother to look back.

Birth

The day you were born,
Eyes opened, both fists clenched,
You were determined
To possess what this wide world
Could give. You wanted
To have what your hands
Could lay hold of. How you cried
To grab what life could offer.
You were born naked
But feeling entitled. Then
They dressed you and pampered you
Like royalty.

Signs of the Times

When the skylarks stop singing
Their joyful, festive songs
To chant the threnodies of death
Over mangled corpses of soldiers
Burnt by the nuclear strikes
Of warring nations, one against another,
No vulture will come, no hyena
Will dare feast on the vanquished
In the valley of desolation;
When the beavers of Lake Tahoe,
Refuse to rebuild their lodges
Or fortify their dams for winter,
Do not bother to look for them,
They are not in hiding; they are all
Dead, killed in the biological warfare
Waged by warring nations, one
Against another, in a travesty of peace
For all people and goodwill to all men,
When hope is drained, and we want out,
He will appear to clean up the mess.

Carlos Prieto González

Seventh of December,
Two thousand and eighteen,
In the year of the Lord,
We visited Iglesia del Carmen,
A past century-old church located
In Getxo, at the slope of Neguri,
Jewel of Bilbao, treasure of Vizcaya.
We went there not to hear
Your down-to-earth homilies,
Simple and well-delivered,
In sonorous spirit-filled Spanish.
It was the eve of your birthday.
We were there to greet you
To demonstrate our love for you.
We were there to celebrate with you
The joy of living together in harmony,
One mind, one heart intent upon God,
The God of our graces who called you
From San Román de los Oteros,
To be a pastor of his flock,
So that from the sanctity of the pulpit
You may remind them of his mercy
And in whatever ministry you perform

You may refract his unfailing love.
Feliz cumpleaños...
Ad multos annos...

Victoriano Valbuena Pinto

Primus inter pares, here you do
Not command, you serve the littlest
Of the flock; *servus servorum Dei*,
You open and close the main door
For those who visit members of our
Observant community; your presence
Fraternal at lauds, at vespers, in all
Of our religious acts; during chapters
You preside; you are the uniting force,
Quiet all the time, intensely listening
To each and every friar present, until
Consensus is reached, and we can
Proceed from one common ground.
Not so far from the Cathedral of León,
Masterpiece of Gothic elegance,
In the fullness of God's chosen time,
From panoramic Quintana del Monte,
God called you, so you may feed
The lambs, with his gospel of love,
The whole community behind your back.

Requiem for Fr. Victoriano Valbuena Pinto, OSA

Un santo varón,
Strong as lion, meek as lamb,
Walked among us. He
Served everyone
When he should be in command.
And he did his best
For the love of God. Christ-like
He brought joy and hope
And spread the gospel of hope
As he sang God's praise.
This *santo varón*
Is now one with God and saints.
Descanse en paz.

Félix Pedro Martín Gómez

Palencia's cathedral leads in antiquity
And shines like its legendary manta
That certainly warmed Jorge Manrique
When he recorded in peerless *coplas*
The one common destiny that claimed
The lives of nobles and royalty
Who once strode the earth in splendor,
The same that will befall all who live
While Ebro River continues flowing
Just as in olden times when in Europe,
Before the flight of the Wright brothers,
It was the center of transport industry.
You *palentinos* are silent workers,
Indestructible like your cathedral,
Deeply embedded in your soul:
"Recuerda el alma dormida…"

We Did Not Go Spelunking

We did not go spelunking
At Miranda Beach.
There was no cave there
To explore, only
Distant ocean,
Threatening, unreachable,
Studded with starfish.
Deep and empyrean.
It was a beautiful day.

So we spent our time
Building sand castles
And catching jellyfish.

Miranda
(For My Brother Romeo)

Landlocked Haguimit,
With no river and no sea,
Made grandma bring us
To Miranda Beach,
Near the house of her cousin,
The first time for you
And for me to watch the waves
Rising and falling
And touching the shore
And back to its source again.
We're past toddlers, still
Below the age of reason.
We asked grandma some questions
About low tide and high tide
At Miranda Beach.

Once the Bridegroom Arrives

Once the bridegroom arrives
– Keep ready, always prepared
And fully awake –
Stand by the front door,
Let in every single guest,
Seat them where they should.
Give them a smile that radiates
Like the chandeliers
That brighten the banquet hall.
With both groom and bride,
Celebrate the victory
Of love faithful and true. Cheers!

Thanksgiving

For your gift of life,
God of all our graces,
All praise and thanksgiving!
For your gift of love,
God of all our graces,
All praise and thanksgiving!
For your gift of wisdom,
God of all our graces,
All praise and thanksgiving!
For your gift of truth,
God of all our graces,
All praise and thanksgiving!
For your gift of justice,
God of all our graces,
All praise and thanksgiving!
For your gift of courage,
God of all our graces,
All praise and thanksgiving!
For your gift of humility,
God of all our graces,
All praise and thanksgiving!
For the gift of joy,
God of all our graces,
All praise and thanksgiving!

For the gift of peace,
God of all our graces,
All praise and thanksgiving!
For the gift of stability,
God of all our graces,
All praise and thanksgiving!
For the gift of prosperity,
God of all our graces,
All praise and thanksgiving!
For the gift of survival,
God of all our graces,
All praise and thanksgiving!

Like a Wounded Disc

Like a wounded disc
The sun is resigned to set.
Empowered, the moon
Stays the course, the stars
Watch like fireflies in hiding,
Awaiting command
From the unseen force
That ordains by day and night
Each single movement
Of this awesome universe,
Beyond what minds of savants
Ever comprehend.

Josephine Dichoso

The so-called way up there can be here,
Not just another dimension to walk into,
But a Shangri-La of peace and quiet
Where the heart beats with contentment
Safe from the clutches of human greed
Somewhere between time and space
Farther than black hole can locate
And siphon out of existence.
You must be there now to sing
With the choirs of seraphim
Never missing one beat, smiling
As you contemplate the Holy Face.

Lorena Ordozgoiti

Yes, there are also angels,
Without wings, visible, they inhabit
The mortal realms where their presence
Shows ailing mankind a glimpse
Of God's grace unfolding
Daily, with infinite patience, star
At night reaching for the farthest end
Of the earth, to give it light, to share
Its comforting radiance for all creatures
To trust in God's mercy, for God's
Love is God's gift to every creature
Who walks the horizon of the earth –
You are that angel. Thanks
Be to God, and God be praised!

Eustaquio Arrausi López

Vitoria strikes me
As a charming city, well
Landscaped, orderly.
Prosperity rules,
And peace reigns in Vitoria,
Your charming city.
Babies and pets stay at home,
And people walk with purpose,
Well dressed, very much prepared
For what lies ahead.
The two cathedrals –
Full, vibrant with believers –
Speak of the people's
Industry, their undying faith
Like the twinkling stars at night
In beautiful Vitoria.

Jesús Buey Redondo

When you sing
Your morning lauds to God,
Distances in light years
Are measured in kilometers
As when you travel by car
From Becerril de Campos,
Your town of three churches,
To Paredes de Nava,
Birthplace of Jorge Manrique
And Pedro Berruguete,
History does not play tricks
On your eagle eye
That can spot heresies
Sparked by winsome doves
Gingerly walking like nuns
Who have made the world
Their wide open cloister.
You move on. At vespers
Your quest for truth reaches
Toward the clear blue sky,
That at night, when you sing,
Is a dome studded with stars,
Attuned to your voice.

Basilio Álava Sáenz

In New York, the Big Apple,
The city that never sleeps,
We whiled our afternoon away
Inside a coffee shop.
We leisurely spent our time
Temporizing poetry.

You encouraged me
To be who I am: a poet.
In between sips of coffee
You told me what you thought
Would make good poetry.
You preferred simple poetry,
Poetry everyone can read,
Poetry anyone can comprehend.

Great poets write
Poems that inspire; timeless
Poems that can pass
The test of time and the many
And relate to all peoples
Of every generation past,
Present, future.

Poems with universal appeal
Are good poetry.

All the while, I was silent.
Every word was an appetizer
For the submarine sandwich
Copiously served afterward,
Touted as the grand enchilada
By that Manhattan coffee shop.

Lauro Rodríguez Mariscal

Love is the safest
Road to holiness, our link
To our Creator,
The new commandment
Christ himself has given, love
Always delivers.
Love never falters.
Crown jewel for all mortals
Who treasure God's reign.
When we look with love
At all our fellow creatures,
We're in love with God.

Francisco Pajares Marcos

In Becerril de Campos,
Verdant patch of fecund earth,
Peace walks unshackled.
Every sparkling pleasant day
Shepherds watch over their flock
Grazing in the sun.
As locals take their siesta
Their charming flower gardens
Cast their fragrant spell
That reaches up the clear sky,
Cloudless any time of day:
Blue. So very blue.

Agustín Pérez Marcos

Tanzania, at first a dream,
You made real when you went there,
First among equals,
Trailblazer of the mission.
You started as a farmer
Sowing gospel seeds
Cobras slithered at your door,
But garlic drove them away
To leave you in peace.
Then you were a fisherman
And you cast your net farther
Down the ocean deep.
You found fellowmen, not whales.
Some volunteered to help you
Spread the love of God.

Ángel Andujar Casañez

In the kingdom of heaven,
To serve is to reign,
To serve is to show
Our love for one another,
The commandment Christ vouchsafed
And demonstrated
For followers to practice
If they freely chose to be
His true disciples.
And this mandate of the Lord
You perform to perfection
By serving us all.

Juan Durán de la Colina

When you joyfully announced
Your grandson Santiago's birth,
We were so happy
Like a patient whose eyesight
Was restored, thanks to your gift
And genius to heal,
Like the mesmerized audience
That watch you perform soothing
Music with your band,
Like the lark that breathes freely
And marvels at the flawless
Handiwork of God.

José María Alonso Alonso de Linaje

Solitude is a true friend,
A companion you can trust
In times of trouble.
When the road gets bumpy,
And you seem to lose your way,
Turn to solitude.
You observe silence: no fuss,
No buzz, not a single word.
Only solitude.
Solitude that just clams up
And helps you find yourself first
And then your way back.

Vicente Jáuregui Presa

So vital in your paintings
Is the element of light.
This light never fails.
Bloody moon in Barrika
Is photo surrealism
Lighted with magic.
Excluded from your paintings
Are wild deer hiding nearby
To avoid the light.
They'll be in your paintings, too,
Once they have the guts to face
The splendor of light.

Federico Albízuri Sagamínaga

In the equation of life,
Right choice equals survival
Between yes or no.
Thus when Javier decided
To visit the Philippines,
He made the right choice.
Your son enjoyed his island
Hopping, and he strangely felt
Drawn to the locals.
He should be: the Philippines
Was evangelized by Basque
Friars of the faith.

Antonio Aguirre Salamero

On the ground of Barrika
Your estate dotted with oaks
I plant this holly
To give you cheerful feeling
Even as the rain may fall
Countless times a day.
The holly may shelter birds
Or give refuge to the bees
Or give joy to those
Who see beauty wherever
God's majesty and glory
Are reflected there.

Rafael Sáenz de Santa María Pombo

So gentle and so noble,
Rafa is an archangel
To all those in need.
The Grupo de Oración,
Of which he is a member,
Is parish jewel.
Swan-necked Isabel, his wife,
Her sister Paz married to
Juan, his brother, the kid
Asís and his bunch of friends
Are all members of this group
Committed to pray unceasingly
For their fellowmen.

Jesús Gregorio Serna Arias

End times may just be around
The corner, and yet we all
Just don't seem to care.
We're on a cruise ship sailing
In the midst of the high seas
We're vaguely informed
That a bomb planted somewhere
May explode anytime soon.
Not all believe it
And those who do keep silent
And live whatever is left
Of their borrowed life.

Policarpo Hernández Fernández

To be free is but to be
What we know we ought to be:
Freedom under grace.
Free to be who we are, free
To fulfill our destiny.
We are God's children –
Loved by God, ransomed by Christ,
Citizens of his kingdom,
Made in his image
And likeness, created as
The pupil of his eye, part
Of God's design.

Félix Urrutia Anda

Happiness does still reside
And glow on ascetic face
As it does on yours
At Lent you interiorize
As you brim with happiness
Which you manifest
In joyful songs that stay
Long after the choir members
Have left their practice.
Your songs bring them to Easter
When they sing alleluia,
Gratefully redeemed.

Cruces

When we talk of Cruces,
Speak of Spain's healthcare
And think of the world's best
Its doctors, some of the Earth's finest,
Its ever-smiling nurses and aides,
Auxiliadores and personnel,
Always ready, never asleep.
From the *escalera de caracol*
See this hospital as a city in itself,
Serving its patients with selflessness.

Luis Casado Espinosa

The inspiring homilies
You deliver to the nuns
Are rich in symbols.
Like the Burgos Cathedral
Where El Cid's remains find rest
They hold them in awe.
Precise, simple, elegant,
Like the sacred cathedral
In Gothic splendor.
And the listeners are moved,
Rapt in ecstatic silence,
Stronger in their faith.

Julián Centeno García

The pectoral cross you wear
Represents Christ, our savior
Who died on the cross
To redeem mankind from sin
And make us heirs of heaven.
The pectoral cross
Must all the time remind us
That Christ came to serve, not to
Be served; that the Christ
Spoke of the forgiving God
And promised us his presence
In the Eucharist.

Javier Antolín Sánchez

God proclaims the innocence
Of all those falsely accused.
Sun rises. Sun sets,
Lightning strikes. Thunder rumbles,
The earth quakes. The sky sheds tears
For the innocent.
Guilt upbraids false accusers
By tormenting them in sleep
With blasted conscience.
God preserves the innocent.
May he keep from harm's way all
Those who uphold them.

Jorge Dulanto Rossi

In my youth, I volunteered
To go to the thick jungle
Of the Amazon.
I feared for my salvation
So I found a way out
Of my assignment:
In an exclusive school where
I could never be myself.
I did not stay long
In Iquitos. Chosica
Was spring perennial.
I went home. Back to square one
And no dull moment.
Of course, you know that Peru
Is more than Machu Picchu.
It could overwhelm.

Alejandro Moral Antón

You're tasked as the General
To merge the four provinces.
You're the right leader:
Unassuming, decisive,
Sturdy and strong like *roble*.
Pursuer of truth
Who knows that in unity
Lies the strength of the Order.
And its survival:
The Augustinian mandate
For all members to follow
To flourish and grow.
For all members to observe
To be relevant.

Cesáreo Miguéliz del Río

The archives of Neguri
Safeguard sacral anecdotes
Of this dainty church,
Shaped like a boat in reverse,
In the volume that you wrote
For posterity
You did not miss anything
Like the fishermen of yore
Who saw the Lady
As their morning star and cast
Their nets, like the disciples
Of the Lord Jesus.

Juan José de la Varga Cano

This room I now occupy,
Well-lighted and well-maintained,
You had occupied
Before you moved to Bilbao
To work at our parish, there
In the city's heart.
As I open the windows
To take a breath of fresh air
I fondly recall
That day we went to Burgos
To pick ripening cherries.
I feel at home here.

Ana María Romo de Miguel

When beauty equals knowledge,
Yet humility prevails,
Silence turns to gold.
Blessed are those who see in you
God's genius as a painter –
Each single stroke a gem.
Because you walk in his ways
And clothe yourself with wisdom
And understanding,
You radiate God's tenderness
As you celebrate his love
And glorify him.

Our Lady of Begoña

Our Lady of Begoña,
Amatxu, little mother,
Walk with us today,
With child Jesus on your knees
And a red rose in your hand,
Lead our pilgrim way.
In darkness or confusion,
In trials or in sorrows,
Free us from false fears.
Our Lady of Begoña,
Patroness of Vizcaya,
Help us persevere.

Miguel Manrique Aparicio

Appointment with destiny
Can't be refused or postponed.
It must be fulfilled
Like pre-arranged tourism
Or unplanned forced vacation.
You're bound to follow.
As you climb up the steep stairs
You see people coming down.
You meet them again
When it's your turn to descend
And they must ascend again
By those very stairs.

Leyenda Negra

Truth chooses to hibernate
In the dungeon of nowhere
Frozen by winter.
In springtime, when the songbirds
Spice the air with their love calls,
Truth stirs back to life.
Walking miles in broad daylight
Diverging in the moonlight,
Truth gathers the strength
To rebound in full glory:
Invincible in autumn,
Fearless and unbound.

Eugenio Alonso Román

Colegio San Agustín
Prepares students for greatness
Through knowledge of God.
It has its own printing press
And a soccer field to train
Peru's future best.
A *vallisoletano*
On a mission to Lima
To proclaim God's Word,
In pure Castilian accent,
Makes of that school *lo mejor*
De los mejores.

Jesús Álvarez Hernández

Bibliographies are needed
To fact-check the black legends
Sired by poisoned pen.
When falsehood spills like virus,
Contagious and venomous,
Bibliographies lead
Us to the primary sources
So we know the difference
Between goose and swan.
Biased pseudo-historians
Create *leyendas negras.*
Unravel them with facts.

Tirso Vega Blanco

When the wicked are gathered
To excoriate the just man,
He's invincible
To their slings of calumny
And their arrows of slander.
The Lord is his shield,
His sun at the break of dawn,
His moon in the pitch-dark night,
All knowing and true.
From the snares of the wicked
And from their insidious lies
God protects the just.

Isacio Rodríguez Rodríguez

So strange are the ways of the Lord,
But men's are more peculiar.
To safeguard world peace
Men must constantly wage war.
They claim God is on their side,
They must have to win.
They slaughter their enemies,
Use God's name to dominate
The submissive ones.
These are some lessons we parse
From your well-documented
Bibliographies.

Pedro Galende García

Urdaneta blazed the trail.
Soon more Augustinians came
To evangelize.
They built churches made of stone.
There they proclaimed the good news
Of our salvation.
Side by side with the natives,
They were like angels in stones.
Love was paid with love.
Urdaneta was long gone
When the seeds he'd sown bore fruit.
Like Urdaneta,
You blazed trails in your own way.
Also, when harvest time came,
You were not around.

Jorge Roldán Moll

The gift of loyal service
Brings peace to the recipient
And to the giver.
It grants manifold blessings
And priceless satisfaction
No money can buy.
This gift of loyal service –
Freely rendered, not for sale –
Sings praise to God's love,
For us: hidden, out of sight.
In spite of our shortcomings,
It's life's saving grace.

Patricia Zazoza Arias

Labor extols God's genius
To create from pure chaos
Or mere nothingness.
He charts stars to stay on course
And planets in their orbit.
He ordains them all.
He gives freedom for mortals
To choose their own destiny
By their own free will.
Steep is the way to heaven
And we must labor real hard
So we can get there.

Santos Abia Polvorosa

From Paredes de Nava
You went to distant China
To spread the good news.
When Mao was swept to power
And his government entrenched,
You were told to leave.
You were sent to Manila
Erstwhile Pearl of the Orient,
Now devastated.
Intramuros in ruins,
Squatters in every corner,
Met your weary eyes.
But then you resolved to stay
To help in the rebuilding
Of that great nation.

Fernando Fernández Fernández

We would take our nightly stroll
Until we reached the seawall
Where we soaked our feet
On the salty seawater.
Counting the stars, we marveled
At God's expertise
To let us live our own lives,
Always free to make a choice
Between good and bad.
When the breeze of the tropics
Started to make us feel cold,
It was time to go home.

José Antonio López Inchaurbe

Before winning the World Cup,
Spain was favored by Arthur,
The psychic *pulpo*
That was promptly invited
By the astonished victors
Euphoric with joy.
In your case there is no need
For any *pulpo* to make
Such a prediction.
You play *futbol*, but your fans
Who tune in to your program
Crown you their champion.

Marimar Aguirre Salamero

To celebrate your birthday,
You invited us for lunch
In a restaurant
That's a magnet for tourists
Who come to sunbathe and swim
On the nearby beach,
Famous for its clean white sand,
Safe for swimming, free from sharks.
We forgot the time.
We did not look at our watch.
We were not interested.
We're just plain happy.

Julio García de la Parte

In *la Amazonia*,
Tied between two giant trees
Swayed a brown hammock.
A woman and her infant
Were there taking their siesta,
Their nose aquiline.
They both opened their dark eyes
As I tiptoed near to them.
They looked welcoming.
In what sounded like Spanish
The mother asked me outright
What I was there for.
I answered by asking her
Why she spoke Spanish. "*Bueno*,"
She said. "*Costumbre*."
In jungle *caseríos*
Of those countries you once worked,
They still speak Spanish.

Madre España

Madre España, land of quixotic charms.
Mother of many nations, cradle of
Conquistadors and innumerable saints,
Unyielding defender of true faith,
Repository of culture,
Custodian of the classics.
Madre España, keeper of just laws,
You keep human rights aflame,
You opened the modern age
Beloved land of El Cid *Campeador*,
Los Reyes Católicos, Carlos I,
Felipe II, Don Juan de Austria,
Madre España, the sun never sets
Where your flag rises red and gold.

LOVE, AND DO WHAT YOU WILL.
— *Saint Augustine*

ILLUSTRATED LOVE POEMS

The Call

When you first called me
I was living in a void,
No way to see you,
No way to respond to you,
There's no way to locate you.
I thought I was just dreaming.
The call got intense
You said you wanted my heart
You said you wanted me to spread
Your love to a world raging with hate.
I was so confused but felt charmed
That you called me by my name
And from out of the dark I rushed
To answer your call.

Communion

Because we love each other
Let us speak only of life
Of what is here and now, on earth.
The fleeting passage to eternity
A quantum leap of realities;
Grandfather's clock, family crest,
Implosion of roses. Pentecost of green,
Nose-diving dragonflies, chirping crickets,
Swans holding back their funeral songs—
Still life, orchestra of the living.
Knowing that you love me for what I am
I cannot but love you for what you are.

Unconditional

You love me for what I am.
Before we even met, you had already loved me
With love beyond reason, with love unconditional.
Far beyond introspection, far beyond the Milky Way,
Farther than space can contain. I am overjoyed
When I think of your all-consuming love, your love
Without beginning, your love without end,
Love ethereal, love most pure, devoid of complications,
Love as simple, as unbreakable as forever.
Who am I to be so loved? Who am I to be
Singled out and chosen? I give you thanks.
In my gratitude, I fully see my nothingness.
Your mighty presence overwhelms,
Gives joy and fulfillment, emboldens me
To sail the uncertain tide of time. Knowing you
Love me as I am is my only reason for survival.

GILBERT LUIS R. CENTINA III

Lullaby of Love

The lullaby of love, a psalmody of life,
Cradles the sun at day and guides the stars at night
The birds of the air frolic on this love
Earth bursts with green to celebrate this love,
This love that awakens roses from their beds,
With butterfly wings from flower to flower
This love that powers ants to work unceasingly
And brings great joy at the birth of a baby
Whose mother sings the lullaby of love
With zeal and tender loving care.

Awake, Dear Heart

Awake, dear heart, the long dark night is over
It is morning, and sunbeams
Stream through the windowpanes
In riots of colors, too dazzling to resist.
The sun is up, a feast for the eyes,
The sky totally clear of ominous clouds.
Violets, irises, carnations and buttercups
All in full bloom, labor of love.
Look even nearer so you can see
This glorious passage of another day.
It's love you're looking for,
It's love you'll surely find.
Protected by fireflies with unerring grit,
Love is unbound for future evenings
When global consumerism and greed
Freeze the heart to indifference.

Triune

Bless you, our Father,
Whose prodigious love for us,
Neither time nor space
Can adequately contain.
Your love glues us together.
Bless you, our Savior,
Whose redeeming love for us
Exacts no frontiers.
Son of God and son of man,
The Way, the Truth and the Life.
Bless you, Paraclete,
The Son's love for the Father,
Dove and tongues of fire,
The Father's love for the Son,
Ever ancient, ever new.

Lord, I Cannot Love You Enough

Lord, I cannot love you enough.
You are so good, so wonderful, so real.
You are so near, yet I cannot follow you
Or fail to retrace your footsteps
As you put order to the universe.
I look at the stars and miss their loveliness
I comb the hills and step on the briars.
I refuse to give up my right of way to peacocks
Strutting like royalty at public parks.
I can't see your face among the Gypsies
Nor figure you out from waves of refugees
Who stampede our shores and jump over our walls
And, spending sleepless days and nights in anxiety,
Hungrily show up with bloodshot eyes
To awaken our conscience but vexing us instead
And so we shoo them off and retweet: *"¡Basta ya!"*

When You Summon Those I Love

And one by one they disappear
Without leavetakings or farewells,
Giving me no time to bid them
Adieu, or hug them and tell them
How much I loved them, how I cherished
Every moment of our togetherness,
How they meant so much to me.
Remembering them only hurts, I drown
In tears of nostalgia, I cease
To be myself. I mourn inconsolably
The loss of those I love.

On This, Our Anniversary

Let me give you my mind,
So forever I can love you;
Please give me your heart,
As I lovingly give you mine.
Between life's stress and storms
We will find the silver linings
Even as we laugh,
Even as we cry,
Never doubting but believing
In the promise of eternity.
Beyond death, I will love you:
In sickness or in health,
In sorrow or in joy.
Let me love you beyond death
Like the way I love you now
Love me no less, now and for always.

And When It Is My Turn to Leave

And when it is my turn to leave
This world of perceptions and uncertainties,
Rejoice and be glad: I'll be in a better place
As I am sure everyone else with faith
Will surely find repose to claim
Mansion of love for those
Who've spent their lifetime in loving
Service, their time with those
Who need their love the most: the outcast,
The poor, the prodigal, the persecuted,
Those deprived of what should have been
Theirs, those denied of justice, condemned
By false witnesses and fake accusers.
I will follow the rainbow and sail
The clouds, tap the silver linings
Behind them, saunter with the man
On the moon. I will follow the trail
Of the milky ways to reach eternity.
Where with vision clear and unerring
I'll watch over you, with loving prayer.

Then There Was Love

So dark, indeed, it was no morning
It was all night, so cold, so uncaring,
So bleak, the heartfelt loss, despairing,
No sign of reprieve, no end in sight
Only total darkness, unfamiliar terrain
Not one to turn to, not one was listening,
The sky was starless, thick clouds forming,
The sun so distant, like light years away
Remorseful claw of regret gripped the heart.
In the midst of darkness, I sought the Lord,
In moment of despair, I held on to my faith.
Darkness faded. The storm passed away.
It was morning,
And then there was love.

Love Struck

Love comes, refuses to identify itself.
It just pops up like an uninvited guest.
Incognito under familiar circumstances
Wearing disguises and retreating
Inside the inmost recesses of the heart,
Palpitating with breathless anticipation
The hidden delight discovery can bring.
As in the framework of the hourglass
Each shred of sand keeps record of time
Swarms of bees pollinate the flowers,
Dews from heaven fructify the earth.
Love is the riddle dangled by the sphinx.

Now

Love me now so you can love me forever:
Now is the moment for me to love you
Now is the moment for you to love me
We both must love each other now
So the promise of eternity may come.
We live in borrowed time; every moment counts,
Every moment is eternity for such as you and me
We claim no ownership of time and space.
This may be the last time for me to see you
Or this may be the last time for you to see me.
We live in borrowed time and space,
Eternity for you and me is now.
Love me now as I love you,
Love me forever and now.
Let us both savor this moment of joy
So we both may partake of eternal bliss.

Confession

Truth to tell... I love you so much.
Mind to mind, heart to heart, soul to soul
From out of the abundance of my heart.
I love you as much as you love me
With love pure and simple and true,
Summer or fall, winter or spring
The bond of our love stronger each time,
Entwined beyond time and space, our hearts
Soar to the pluriverse of the unknown,
In an acrobatic display of enduring love
The portal of eternity within our grasp.
Truth to tell.

Greetings

How do you do?
Still remember me?
Once in a while, I remember you.
Once in a while, I don't.
I live for the day.
There are so many choices to make,
There are so many risks to take.
Who knows what will happen next?
I still travel a lot like what we used to do.
Who can guess what's in the pilot's mind?
Who can tell if the plane will crash?
Who can tell if the boat will sink?
Walking down the street has its own hazard, too.
Some warrior of an angry god
May just plow unsuspecting tourists
To their bloody death.
Parroted by icons of immorality
News we hear can be fake –
How do you do?
After all these years, I still love you.
After all these years, I still love you.

I, a Time Traveler Who Loves You

I, a time traveler who loves you,
Affirm my love for you, again
And again, God of all our graces,
Giver of life, our destination,
Pilot of our spaceship, the Earth:
I thank you for your gift of life,
For giving me the will to live.
Grant me faith, steadfast and true
Let me survive when the soul
Is put to test, as gold in a furnace,
By the angel with the flaming sword
That claims mortals in their sleep
And lays them beyond infinity
Where death exists no longer.
Because life is no more.
Where only love prevails.

Yes, I Sought Refuge in You

Nothing here to brag about.
All the reason to love you completely
And to tell you how really grateful I am
For everything you've done for this
One graceless child, at times incredulous,
At times failing to remember that you,
Who ordain the courses of the stars
And guide the movements of the planets,
Are the beginning and the end,
The compass for time travelers
Whose spaceship is the Earth.
Lord of our graces, thank you
For your mercy and forgiveness,
Thank you for your gift of love.

Every Which Way

When they told me
That I should never love you at all
And that you should never love me either
For reasons far longer
Than the litany of saints,
Dire like the predictions
Of end-time visionaries
Who claim access to the Divinity
And use God's name at every opportunity.
Cackling like hens in the midst of a storm,
Looking for a grain of sand in a haystack.
I closed my eyes to see nothing.
I covered my ears to hear nothing.
I said nothing.

Knowing That You Love Me

Knowing that you love me
And telling me in uncertain terms
Mine are the best things in life
By you freely given, with love,
With compassion gifts gratuitous
From you, the source of love
From the very beginning and beyond
Love so pure and love so divine
Love that endures, love that survives,
Core of my being. My only love.

I Would Not Trade

I would not trade anything for heart
That wants to love but suffers for
That love: ridiculed, derided,
Scorned and mocked behind the back
Of same someone who dared to love
And wished to be loved in return.
The heart cannot take so much suffering.
Once broken, the heart finds it hard
To heal itself again. As grief takes over,
Joy vanishes, life refuses to move on.

When You Love

When you love, give your whole heart
To someone you are pledged to love,
Without reserve, without doubt, without
Any anxiety or fear, without suspicion,
Trusting and honest to someone fate
Destines to live with you forever.
Give love that will rattle
The nadir of the netherworld
Where lost souls end up,
And touch the apex of the stars,
In the corridor of virtues.
Give your whole heart. Give love.

Elegy for Comet

Brownie, the rabbit
Gave up the ghost one morning.
Unforgiving, the winter
Chilled us to the bones
And filled us with grief.
Like you, Brownie was a joy.
When the tulip bed opened
To find rest for our dear pet
And as I said some prayers
You watched my every movement.
Touched, I whispered in your ear
"You're the best dog in the world."

Summer's here, and as you go
To join Brownie, the rabbit,
I shout to the world: "Comet,
You're the best dog in the world!"

To Love You Is a Gift

To love you is a gift,
Gratuitous and rare,
Like the air I breathe.
I can find it anywhere,
But only where it matters,
But only where it counts most,
Like rarest orchid and choicest grass
In the garden of my faith.
I must take care of this gift,
Watch it prosper, see it bloom,
Nourish it with gratitude,
Shower it with best of care,
Treasure it in my heart,
Mine and mine forever.

True Love

I love you; you belong to me.
I am yours; we both exist
To love each other, honor each other,
Pursue together one path in life,
Not parallel, but united by the bond
Of love: free, unwavering, willing
To roll up our sleeves to survive
The daily onslaughts of vicissitudes.
You love me; I belong to you.
I am yours; we both exist
To live only for each other,
We both know it fully well.

Love

I am love. You need not ask where
I come from. I am love. Spring, summer,
Autumn, winter. I am love. In stress
And storm, I am love. In peace and quiet
I am love. When all seems, lost I am love.

When faith remains, I am love,
At the break of day, I am love.
At the setting of the sun, I am love.
In joy and in pain, I am love.

Like earth carpeted in green,
Like sky, immense dome of blue,
Like recyclable ocean waves.
I am deathless. I am love.

ACKNOWLEDGMENTS

This book would not have been possible without the unflinching support of friends and family, especially my Augustinian brothers in Loiu, Bilbao, and Neguri. Their fraternal love, generosity, and random acts of kindness have sustained me. My deep appreciation of their friendship and tender gestures are memorialized in some of the poems in this collection. Because of their unconditional support, I can pursue my priesthood of literature unfettered.

A special debt of gratitude is owed to Machús Aguirre, an extraordinary artist whose illustrations make this poetry collection remarkable. Born in Bilbao, Spain, she is the third in a wonderful large family that always encouraged her to develop her artistic talent. Machús studied journalism at the University of Navarre. Before abandoning journalism in favor of painting, among other pursuits, she worked for two regional newspapers. She later became a correspondent for a national newspaper in Spain.

She began to paint with acrylic and oil after participating in outdoor painting competitions in Pamplona, where she was selected for the final exhibition on two occasions. A member of the Artistic Society of Guipúzcoa in San Sebastían, Spain, where she currently lives, she loves painting portraits and landscapes in brilliant colors.